The Mind, The Body

ALYSSA HUBBARD

Alyssa Hubbard

ISBN: 1499683367
ISBN-13: 978-1499683363

DEDICATION

This is dedicated to my brother and sister.
Yes, you guys. Your sister is just as crazy as
you think she is.

ALYSSA HUBBARD

MORE BY ALYSSA HUBBARD

Humans and Their Creations

Apocalyptia (Apocalyptia Series #1)

An Austrian March

CONTENTS

ACKNOWLEDGMENTS

Once again, I am honored to have a book cover made by the wonderful Cover Bistro. You rock, Jes. I must also take a moment and thank Andrea for all her help reading these stories and making suggestions. You've inspired me more than you know.

1 – HETEROCHROMIA

I was born in a family of five blue-eyed, blonde-haired southern gentlemen. My mother was decidedly absent for most of my life, having been one of the foolish sort, often times putting too much into her own silly superstitions than what they were worth. She was highly dedicated to the Lord's word and could often be found praying as she went about her menial tasks. Even the regular obstacles of life sent her into a fit of prayer. But it was a minor annoyance my father had traded for hot meals and sons. As long as she remained useful, he would bare anything to keep her around. My brothers had to deal with it as they grew, but when she had born me in the loft of father's barn, on a night when the rain pounded the rotted wood and drenched the hay until it too smelled of death and rot, no one would have to listen to her prayers again.

The barn, for her, had become a church. It was the only building with a second story, and the closer she was to God, the better. Father didn't stop her, even if it stormed. The man had preached to her, hoping to sway her, but she wouldn't have any of it. It felt too isolated in the house for her. She wanted to have her children where God could see, so the abandoned barn with its cracked ceiling, shuttered windows, and the scent of livestock which never completely went away was where we had all been born. Yet, I would be first baptized in that very same loft.

The night of my birth, she gazed upon my golden head with the love of every mother who had ever existed, cooing and holding me close to her pale bosom. I was her first and only daughter. The first she would be able to teach the Lord's word to day-in and day-out. I'm sure she had dreams for me, dreams which she had saved just for the day she finally birthed a daughter. It was finally here, all her praying finally come to fruition. She begged to see my eyes, to look into their never-ending blue depths and to see all her love emulated into a single human creation, and when I opened my eyes she found:

One blue.

One green.

She prayed hard that night. Prayed as she left a little, soaked bundle in the loft, wrapped in nothing but a fragment of saddle cloth from a horse my father had put down some months ago. Perhaps she had wanted me put down, too. Perhaps she thought I was some creature born from her sins – not of love, but of atonement. Regardless, it was the last I saw of my mother. It was the last *anyone* had seen of my mother.

And amongst the men, I grew. My father came for me in the early morning. He thought nothing of my eyes, but rather worried more for my health. It would be foolish to think he did so in the name of parental affection. He cared not whether I lived or died, but what he did worry about was the planting of his crops and the care of his farmland. If he were to keep me alive, would I survive only to lead a life of fragility and be unable to even keep the house? It would be a heavy burden to care for a daughter who would never be able to marry and do the basic task of womanhood. If I showed a hint of weakness, he would take me back into the barn loft. It was an archaic form of euthanasia, one which was often left for the dogs and sick livestock. That was what I was to my father – an asset, minor livestock to be raised and to eventually benefit the family. My death would have been a loss, no matter how minor my worth truly was, and he could only hope that my survival would be a gain.

I can't hate him for it. The life of a farmer is a hard one, without the added frustrations of a sickly child. But I could certainly never love him for it, either. It didn't rightly matter. My father wasn't of the loving sort. Once I had proven my worth, living in and out of that loft for the first portion of my young life, and never once catching illness, even during the heaviest of downpours, I was brought into the house. It wasn't long after that I was bullied back to it – to seek sanctuary from the torment of my brothers, my teachers, and my classmates. Even the animals had begun to torment me. I felt it in the way they watched me as I walked through the fields. Their blank gazes followed me from dawn till dusk, and never did they get close enough for me to touch. They wouldn't come near their hay until I'd left it, and even then they barely touched it. It had escalated to the point that they would stop eating all together. My brothers said the hay smelled of death when I touched it, and the animals could smell it, too.

The eye – the single green eye was the physical creation of my torment. Even when I slept, in the darkness I could feel it lurch about in my skull. It was alive, you see. It did what it wanted. Some nights, I awoke in the middle of the night to a burning sensation in my left eye – *that* eye. It would burn and simmer, like a festering sore inside my

4

skull. Could you imagine? Having a boil burning inside your head? Why did I suffer nightly because of it?

The eye *looked* at things. During the night, it opened of its own accord, and would simply look. It wouldn't blink. It wouldn't close. It would open and gaze out into the night until it dried out, which would then wake me. The only nights of peace I ever received were when it rained. My eye could open and watch and the rain would hydrate it again.

But that had only been the beginning of my torment. It had taken on a life of its own, it had developed a voice – one which seemed to echo in my brain and bounce about in my skull.

It would whisper, "Dream not through the night."

And I would plead, "No, Devil. I wish to sleep. Why must you torment me so?"

"Your sleep will be wrought with fears. We must pray."

"No, no! I will not hold council with you, Devil. Leave me to rest."

But the eye never would rest. It continued on with its ramblings until I could hardly tell my own thoughts from those of the eye. The rambling ranged from prayer to pleas, and once those prayers slipped into my waking hours, I knew something needed to be done. I was becoming like my mother, a paranoid zealot. As I prayed in the field, I swore to myself and to God that I would be rid of my demon – my mother – once and for all.

It was a disgusting act, and it could all be traced back to my birth. Back to when my mother left me to soak in the rain. My first night alive on this planet, and the woman who carried me for nine months left me in the soaked hay to rot in the rain. Was I not worth those nine months? Had my conception and birth truly been for nothing? *She* had been the one who created me. *She* had been the one to make the *eye*. Why did I have to suffer for the sins of my mother?

Was that why she feared me so? Because she feared herself?

But it didn't matter. The water, the thing which I had survived and found comfort in, had cleansed me and my eye. Cleansed it so I could see what needed to be done. There was one night, when the rain began to pour and my right eye opened to join my left in its vigil that I became truly aware of what needed to be done. The lightning danced above like chains in the sky and lit my loft until it was filled with the strangest shadows. In the night I listened closely and heard the steady thrum of the blood within my body and the heart in my chest. My body was telling me something. My body was revolting against the devilish organ held within my socket. My body wanted to rid itself of the green boil inside my face, and I was happy to oblige. It was during that night, as I soaked in the rain and breathed in the heavy scent of manure and wet hay that I truly studied my body, and from there I made my plan.

The next morning, I sent my eldest brother to town with every penny I had. He pitied my unfortunate soul and did what I asked of him with little questioning. I was beyond grateful. I couldn't go out in public. Not until it was done. He came back that evening with what I most desired, but had most feared. It was a tiny hand mirror, encrusted in silver metal which had begun to tarnish green – a fitting color, I decided. The glass itself was completely intact, and that was all I had cared about. It would do for my task. Yet, what had begun to haunt me more so than the eye was that of my own reflection. I did my best to avoid meeting my own gaze, but my curiosity always managed to lure me in, and throughout my morning chores I would find myself sliding the mirror from my pocket to study my visage.

I was a woman. There was no question about it. I don't wish to seem prideful, but if I had been born without the eye, my father would have had no problem finding a husband for me. My cream skin was tinted honey, a shade which was uncommon amongst the burnt farmer daughters. My hair had been bleached white from years toiling out in the sun when most of my female peers had been kept indoors. I was more than a farmer's daughter, I was exotic. Yet, as beautiful and exotic as I appeared, all who I came in contact with feared me. Perhaps I was feared for more than just my eyes – though they were a sight to behold, too. They had bags beneath them, one of the few flaws to be found, but when gazing into them, first blue, then green, I found myself hypnotized. I decided then it was some form of witchcraft or magic and promptly stopped myself from looking any longer. I wouldn't. Not until it was time.

Night seemed to crawl into the day, and I waited anxiously in my loft once my chores had been completed. I set the mirror up on hay bales I had stacked during the day. I needed it to be my station. Before the sun had completely disappeared, I fumbled in the hay and the darkness where I found my candle, wrapped in the very saddle cloth which had kept me alive at my birth. It was special, that way. I lit the wick and set the candle beside my mirror. Within seconds I heard the soft shuffle and clatter of my brother with dinner. He clambered up the ladder, loud, but silent. He simply slid the tray across the floor and I listened a bit longer for him to slide down the ladder and fumble out of the barn again, leaving me once more in silence.

I felt my way over to the tray and pulled it to my work station where I studied it under the candle light. It was chicken of some kind, though I could scarcely make out its shape. The dim light of the candle casted a shadow over the meal, darkening the meat until it looked like something more. Like a child, perhaps? I plucked up the silverware and held it close to the candle. A knife and a spoon were my tools, and the latter was what I chose. With my remaining utensil, I stabbed the shadowy chicken and watched a blackened fluid pour from the wound. I couldn't tell if it was blood or juices. I took it as an omen and my body physically wilted at the impending surgery which I was about to perform.

It was too late. I had gone too far to stop, and my resolve was strengthened by the cacophony of thunder above. I rested my meal in my lap, clenched the spoon, and gazed into the mirror. It would be the last time I looked in the mirror and saw my face as it had been. I lifted the spoon to my face and pressed the chilled metal against my bottom eyelid. Sweat and cold metal will forever be the most frightening of combinations, and it would haunt me for years to come. I took in a shaking breath, then shoved in the spoon.

It was a searing pain at first. My body writhed and revolted against the intrusion, more so than it ever had over the very organ which I was scooping from my socket. My hand twitched with agony and heated trails of blood warmed my cheek. I wanted to stop. I wanted to pull it out and start over, but I couldn't. I had to pull out the eye first. My heart was thrumming even harder in my chest which only made it harder to breathe. I was going to faint. As dark as it was in the loft, nothing could compare to the darkness which intruded my mind, gradually covering my brain with a fuzzy mold which made it hard to even think.

The thunder cheered above, right before a steady stream of rain began to pour in. It cooled my flesh and washed away the blood. My body seemed to calm at its arrival. I took in one breath, another, and another, then I began at my work again, determined to finish what I had started. I would succeed. I tried to look into the mirror, to steady my work, but my vision had blurred to the point I couldn't see through the darkness.

I shut my blue eye and scooped. With a rush of air the spoon came free, and for a moment I felt a slight pull, then nothing. A fleshy blob plopped against the skin of my cheek, and all was silent except for the gentle pitter patter of the rain above. I couldn't really *feel* the eye, but there it was, warming my cheek and occasionally tugging from the force of the rain. All that was left between me and the bane of my existence was a string of flesh. All I had to do was break it, and I would be free. But for a split second, I felt the urge to push the eye back into place. Perhaps the eye was more powerful than I had ever imagined, or perhaps it was my own fear coming back to haunt me. I could fix it if I wanted to. I could start over and all would be well. It was a feeling so jarring, my hands trembled with anticipation, and the spoon clattered to the floor, slipping from my grip. Could it be pushed back in? I raised my hand as if to try, but then I thought of that damn eye and its demands. I couldn't let that thing win.

I gripped the fleshy pulp in my hand and yanked it free.

The moment it was separated from the cord, I felt an intense rush of nausea, and I was wrought with the image – or perhaps a memory – of my mother pulling me free from her, screaming and writhing in a world of rain and lightning.

The organ plopped into the plate at my lap. I focused my remaining eye there just in time for a strike of lightning to illuminate the loft so I could see my blood mixing amongst the juice and the meats. There was no way I could tell the difference. I had lost my appetite.

Then I gazed into the mirror. All I could see was the smudge of my silhouette amongst the darkness. I needed another flash of lightning. One more and I could see my freedom. The result of my operation would finally be revealed to me. I needed to know it was all truly finished. I would be normal. I would *finally* be normal.

Oh, but what a fool I was.

The lightning flashed.

I met my gaze in the mirror, and where my green eye had been there was now a gaping hole in my skull. Darkness returned and all fell silent once more. I reached up to my face and slid a finger into the cavern. Empty – it was totally empty. I had mutilated myself. Rather than carry the burden of a different eye, I had performed the ultimate sin: I had destroyed God's creation. Perhaps it hadn't been my mother's sin which I had carried. Perhaps it had been my own. Or worse yet, perhaps it had been a gift. What had I done? My heart didn't thrum, my body didn't writhe. I just sat there: numb.

Then, within the silence, I could hear the voice of a woman echoing within the confines of my socket. My mother, I assumed. She was praying.

"Please, Lord. Forgive me for not trusting in your plan. You have given me the task of raising a child with such a gift, but I cannot. My fears will not let me, though I know you have a reason for it all. Have mercy on my weak soul, and on her blessed one. Please don't let her suffer, and please do not let her become me."

I let out a sob and lay on the hay. It no longer smelled of death, but instead had taken on the aroma of blood and viscera. I was deafened by what sounded like the cry of a newborn. I didn't realize it was my own voice fading into the downpour until I finally allowed my consciousness to disappear completely.

And for the first time since my birth, I slept.

2 – THE PIANO PLAYER

She lived just down the street from the hospital. Night shifts and silence were the usual as she walked from work to home, home to work, then back again, but as she stepped out into the night air, she was pressed with unease. Beads of sweat formed at her brow, even as the night air whipped around her. She shook herself and started on her walk back to her apartment.

Very few cars passed her along the way, and even fewer drove slow enough to allow her the reprieve of their headlights as she continued to move like a shadow in the darkness. The closer she was to her apartment building, the warmer her forehead grew and the sweat had already begun to drip into her eyes. She ran her coat sleeve across her face, but only managed to catch a few beads. The dim lighting from the windows cast an eerie glow across the sidewalk and leaked out into the street. Any other night she would've been relieved to see the beacons, but what the light revealed scared her more than what she couldn't see within the darkness.

A man stood outside the building, his features covered with a thick mustache and beard. His nose formed a beak above the hair and his eyes were hooded by thick, yellowing lids. His lips protruded from his face as if swollen, and even in the dim light, she could still make out the cracks and grooves which seemed to cover the pinkish skin. He wasn't tall, the top of his bald head barely reached the windows of the entry doors, but his body was round and cut into sharp angles by the thick jacket he had draped around his body. She couldn't recall ever seeing him before, though his identity was the least of her worries. He paid little attention to her as she side-stepped him to get into the building, and for that she was grateful.

Inside the main entry way to the building, her shoulders dipped and she let out a rush of air. Her body warmed in the brightly lit room, and the sweat which formed at her brow froze and chilled the heated flesh. It was silent except for the constant whir of the tiny fan the manager kept at the service counter. He wasn't there, which was unusual, but she assumed he had gone on to bed for the night. It wouldn't be long until the morning manager came in to take his place. As the night wore on her body, and the adrenaline left her empty, she dug into her pocket and procured a ring of keys: one for her apartment, the other for her mail box. Her eyes drifted over to the mail boxes, lined up into a neat little block of around twenty other occupants. Had she checked the mail before she left for work? She couldn't recall and the ache in her shoulders told her it wasn't worth checking, but she decided it would be best to get the sting of bills over with.

She trudged toward the boxes, key already poised. She stopped just in front of them and put the key into the lock of box 16. The key caught. It took a bit of jiggling before it would turn, but it eventually glided around until it clicked and the little door popped free of its latch. She didn't even have to open the door all the way to see the first bill poking out, its red lettering blaring against the white envelope. With a groan, she pulled out the mail and slammed the little door shut before yanking out her keys. She stuffed it all into one of her pockets and smiled at the satisfying crunch. She was beyond ready for the day to be over, but her weariness gave way to fear as she turned around and found the man from outside standing in the middle of the room, his gaze locked on the elevator across from the entrance.

She crumpled the mail in her pockets, gripping the paper until it formed a ball. The man didn't move, except for the occasional glance in her direction and the constant smacking of his chapped lips. His head didn't move. He kept his body and head facing the elevator, only his eyes cut towards her. She swallowed and glanced at the elevator then toward the stairwell, a few feet away. She entertained the idea of taking the stairs for a while, but by the time she had decided it was the best option, her gaze shifted back to the man, only to discover *he* was looking toward the stairwell. This had the sweat moving down her face again, and her gaze was stuck back on the elevator.

Though she hated to, she started the walk toward the elevator, grateful to find that her footsteps were the only ones to be heard echoing in the empty building. She pressed the button, finger slipping against the plastic. Had the elevator always taken so long? She counted:

One…

Two…

Ding.

As soon as the doors slid open, she rushed in. In the safety of the elevator, she clicked the button to her floor, floor 9, then stepped all the way to the back to watch the man as the doors took their time to close. The doors had nearly closed by the time her heart began to calm and she was hit with the weight of the night. Her fist relaxed in her pocket, releasing the paper ball which had once been her mail and leaving her with an aching throb against her palm. She pulled her hand from her pocket and examined the key-shaped indent left in her skin.

Distracted by the pain, she hadn't noticed the man rush to the elevator, and right before the doors could fully shut, he thrust the handle of his umbrella into the narrow opening. She let out a yelp and froze. The doors locked onto his umbrella, and time stood still. The man peered through the crack of the doors and stared directly at her, smacking his lips as he did. She could only focus on keeping her breathing steady. Eventually, the doors opened back up, and the man casually entered the elevator. He opted to stand in the middle and clicked the button for his floor with the tip of his umbrella, floor 10. She was grateful he had decided to distance himself from her, but being trapped in cramped quarters with him did nothing to comfort her.

The smell of him was nauseating. He filled the elevator with the scent of poppies, and the woman couldn't recall ever smelling such a perfume before. She did her best to filter the smell by pressing the sleeve of her jacket against her mouth and nose, but even her own clothing seemed saturated with the odor and the taste. He never turned around to study her, and he never attempted small talk. The silence left the woman with little to do except to study the strange man further. The fact that he carried an umbrella perturbed her as it hadn't rained in weeks, and in the middle of winter it was unlikely that it would for another few months. She also took note of his gnarled hands, which twitched as he held them against his sides. In the pocket on the same side he clutched his umbrella, there was a crumpled bouquet of paper. Something was written on it, but it wasn't words. The woman squinted her eyes and found the paper wasn't lined as proper writing paper would be, but instead had bars, like a music score. Upon further scrutiny she found it was peppered with handwritten music notes and dynamics, clumsily scratched in and barely landing on the lines. The man was a musician of some sort. She didn't have a chance to inspect further as the elevator halted and the doors opened to reveal her floor.

With a sense of relief, the woman rushed by the small man and took a sharp left, leaving the elevator far behind. She didn't stop her hurried steps until she had made it safely to her door. Once there, she removed her keys and shoved them into the door's lock. The lock caught, and the women sighed as she nervously peeked over her shoulder. The hall was empty.

She took in a deep breath and looked to the lock where she had to jiggle the key before it would glide into place and allow the knob to turn. She made her way inside her apartment, threw her keys into the glass bowl beside the door, then made sure to close and lock the door back before heading to her bedroom. She didn't waste any time and immediately got into bed, coat and all. Her body sagged into the bed, the full weight of the day finally sinking in, but before she could drift off to sleep, she heard the faint sound of music being played above her head. She sat up and looked to the ceiling, listening to the careful and precise notes of the piano on the next floor. She smiled, then lay back down to fall into a deep slumber.

The woman awoke not too long after to find the music still playing above her head and the patter of rain outside her bedroom window. She sat up, dazed and empty. The woman rose from her bed, her form limp and wobbling. She couldn't recall ever feeling so drunk before in her life. She made her way out of the bedroom and into the foyer, where she eyed her small balcony, something she paid $30 extra for every month.

Rain poured in sheets outside, and the railings of the

small balcony couldn't be seen from where she stood. Struck with curiosity, she made her way outside. She opened the glass door and stepped onto the balcony. The rain soaked her coat within seconds, and her limp body sagged beneath its weight, but she trudged on. Despite the downpour, she could still hear the faint sound of the piano growing louder and louder above her until it seemed to meld in with her thoughts and come from inside her somewhere. She walked further and further forward until her knees bumped into the squat railing of the balcony. Yet the music continued to grow in speed and intensity.

All she had to do was lean forward. Just a bit more and she'd be over the railing. She did, and with the help of the rain and the weight of her coat, her feet lifted from the safety of the concrete within seconds. She fell nine floors in a glorious crescendo and crumpled on the ground beneath. Then, all was silent.

In the pocket of Janet Burroway's jacket was a crumpled newsletter from a local occult magazine, mixed in with her regular bills. The newsletter specifically mentioned the 10-year anniversary of the Piano Player Suicide. The piano player mentioned was John Martin, an aspiring musician and composer. He committed suicide on his 50th birthday after receiving a diagnosis of arthritis, which hindered his ability to perform as well as write music. He threw himself from the tenth floor balcony of the same building Janet Burroway lived. He died upon impact. Janet Burroway was said to be healthy, happy, and an outgoing young woman. There was no history of suicide in her family or in her youth. Investigators continue to question neighbors and the managers of the building, but there is no evidence of foul play. The suicide of the musician and that of Mrs. Burroway remain unconnected.

3 – THE WOLF COVERED IN RED

Once upon a time, there was a young wolf that lived in a cottage with his mother, father, and siblings. They were simple wolves, hunting only what meat they needed and could store for the winter months. They hardly ever encountered humans and never trespassed on human territory. Humans were for the desperate, and they were not desperate. They lived together happily for many years, until humans encountered *them*. Hunters and woodsmen began moving in and clearing out their territory, edging closer and closer, but sparing the wolves. They lived happily once more in isolation.

But as times grew harder and their hunting grounds grew more and more sparse, the wolves became much more desperate in their efforts to stay alive - to live as they had in the world before humankind. The humans treaded on their land and hunted the very prey they had subsisted on for so long. Even the fruits and vegetation were at the mercy of the people. Just as quickly as the fawn weaned and the carrots sprouted, they were taken with nothing left behind for the following seasons.

Eventually, the forest they had hunted for generations and generations was left barren. The wolves could no longer prosper, much less survive on what was left. The wolves that were once kindly and gentle had become desperate. In December, the cold took the father. In spring, the flu took the mother. The young wolf, the eldest of the three siblings was left to provide for all the remaining family. He was just as desperate as his mother and father had been, but he did his best to retain what little dignity his family had maintained.

They had a separate family pack just on the other side of the forest named the Other Wood, and rumors had spread of it being one of the few remaining prosperous wolf packs. His grandmother and grandfather had been a part of that very pack. The young wolf wasn't sure if they were still there or not, but the rumors were too tempting to ignore. They had a stock of their own, had their own gardens lush with vegetables, and all untouched by humankind. The young wolf was just desperate enough to travel through human country to get to it, and he prayed he wouldn't come back an even more desperate animal. So, he packed a single sack with what little provisions his family could spare, said his goodbyes, and began the trek to the Other Wood.

The journey started off fairly simple, on a dirt road through the woods the young wolf had been raised in. Once rolling mounds of earth, grass, and trees which had formed canopies above the heads of the travelers, merchants, and woodland creatures that passed through, now was desert. The green grass and brown earth were charred a dark gray, an ash, most likely. The trees had lost their leaves, and were like brown, wilted tombstones rooted in the ash. The sun burned the remaining brush and the dirt road seemed more like dust. The ground kicked up around the young wolf in a cloud as he walked, and the sun made it all that much more uncomfortable. The young wolf prayed, and he prayed hard, and the clouds did move to dim the sun. He was thankful, and continued on his way.

During his travels, he came upon a young girl, coated in a thin hood and cape of red wool. The young wolf thought she was manic for wearing such warm clothing out in the heat, but they were people, and they had their own ways about them. The young girl couldn't be any older than he was, around fourteen or fifteen, yet the way her cheeks sucked in and the bags beneath her eyes purpled by the second the wolf thought she could have been forty if she wanted to be. The young girl was completely alone, save for the young wolf and a small wicker basket she clutched within her bony, gray hands.

The wolf asked her,

"Where are you going?"

The young girl smiled, though the black little nubs did not a smile make. Her voice was hoarse and it crackled as she spoke. She said,

"To my grandmother's house for tea and cakes. Where are you going?"

The mere mention of food, even of the human variety, had the wolf salivating. He prayed about it, but the thought of pastries and warm tea never did leave him. He tried his best to keep on the subject,

"To my grandmother's house, as well." He smiled, "She has many treats for me and my family in the Other Wood."

The young girl looked surprised, her cloudy blue eyes wide like saucers. Then she asked,

"You have family?"

The wolf nodded and replied,

"Yes, don't you?"

The young girl pursed her lips, and the wolf was

thankful. The little black nubs would haunt him for many nights, he was sure. The young girl was silent for a long time and the wolf was beginning to sweat beneath the heat as morning waned and the afternoon began to take hold. He couldn't wait much longer. He had to get to his grandmother's house before night fall. Finally, the young girl shook her head, a furious motion which caused the hood of her frock to slide from her head, revealing patches along her scalp of stringy yellow hair. The little strings barely moved as she shook, and the wolf did his best to not stare, but he couldn't bring himself to look away. The little girl didn't seem to notice.

"No. No siblings." The young girl looked down the road, as if she was seeing something far, far away. "I had two, but they aren't here now."

She pursed her lips again, and it was clear the conversation was over. The young wolf was preparing to say goodbye when she flashed another grin of black stones and said,

"Why don't we travel together? We're both going to the Other Wood!"

He wasn't sure if it was the right thing to do, but the prospect of companionship along his travels did draw him in. It would be safer for the both of them, he decided to himself. Yet, the fear of his desperate side still lingered over him. He wasn't worried for himself. Though weakened he was from the lack of proper nutrition, the little girl in red posed no threat to him, which only made her that much more alluring. Whichever half of him decided, there was no telling, but he decided right then,

"Of course we can."

The young girl giggled and said nothing more as they began again on their path to the Other Wood. It wasn't until they had already started walking that he realized she had never mentioned where her grandparents lived. He guessed it had slipped her mind, though he couldn't be sure.

After the sun had waned and dipped low enough to touch the earth, the wolf and the girl decided to stop for the night. The wolf hadn't packed a sleeping bag or tent, assuming he would've made it to his grandparents' by nightfall, but there was no other choice for his weakened body. The girl huffed and pushed him to go further.

"There's a city not too far from here. We could get a room and a hot meal from those humans."

But the wolf couldn't go further, and the young girl in red was ignored. She didn't complain and settled in on the ground beside the wolf as he lay down, too. The young wolf did his best to sleep, but found he was unable to settle comfortably on the hard, dusty ground. He tossed and turned, all while the little girl in red slumbered peacefully at his side. Within only a few hours, the wolf gave up on sleep and settled for thinking. He thought about his siblings, how they were doing, if they were okay, if they were hungry or starving. Then he wondered if he was starving.

He ran a hand down his stomach, the sunken flesh dipping low. He hadn't eaten in a long time. His bag was right beside him, but he couldn't bring himself to eat while the young girl beside him slept. Then his thoughts honed in on the girl, and his gaze went with them. He wondered how often she ate. Judging by her size, not very much, but his mind led him somewhere else. He wondered how much he could eat *off* of her, how she would taste, and how long it would take to chew through her throat. He was growing desperate, and it scared him more than the girl had. He knew there would be no chance of sleeping that night.

The young wolf watched the sunrise, and the little girl stirred. When she woke, there was no time for breakfast, only time to move. Her enthusiasm was refreshing, though unwanted, as the young wolf feared the sweet smell of her youthful energy, which seemed to come from her in waves. He was beginning to regret ever allowing her to join him on their journey, but there was no turning back. They moved along.

The girl had been right about the city, not far from where they had stayed, and the young wolf was in shock at how bustling and loud it seemed compared to the crippled forest just along its edges. There were trees - real, living trees at the center of the city, as if for some kind of park or field. People rode around in cars and other strange modes of transportation the young wolf had only ever heard of in storybooks. And the people - they were everywhere. They were milling through the streets in never-ending streams, coming in and out of buildings and skyscrapers. It was the closest to an ocean the young wolf had ever seen.

Though he thought it beautiful, something about how isolated the little city was had his stomach turning. How would they react to a wolf coming into a city with a young and defenseless girl? That many people? He wouldn't last but a few minutes, and that would be if they gave him a head start. Despite all of his inner-turmoil, the girl in red was far from worried. She took the young wolf's paw and yanked him down to the city, with no warning and no chance for him to say otherwise. Before he could even ready himself, the girl had pulled him into the throng.

The wolf found the voices deafening, even as the people closest to them froze and silenced. As they milled through the people, the closest groups stopped and took stock of the couple. It was unnerving having a bubble of silence around them when only moments ago the wolf couldn't even hear his own thoughts. And their gazes? They were afraid, understandably so. The young wolf could already tell they hadn't seen a wolf before, or if they had it had been of the desperate variety.

He swallowed. That's how they were looking at them - like they were the desperate wolves. The young wolf had made that same expression plenty of times, but he had never had it pressed onto him, especially by humans. His eyes drifted over to the girl who continued to drag him through the people, paying no mind to any of the reactions around her. They might as well have not existed. He wondered if she didn't care or if she just didn't notice. The more he tried to ignore it, the more apparent it became. Some of the people even looked sad or sympathetic. He hated that look more than the fear.

He was thankful when they had made it through the city, back in the ruined woods. Though he didn't look back to see, the people of the city all stood vigil and watched the pair fade away in the dust of the woods. They seemed to be mourning, though it didn't last long. Once the pair had disappeared from view, the milling continued. Life started again.

It took only that morning to finally arrive at the young wolf's grandparents', and once that lovely home came into view, the young wolf all but screamed with joy. He and the girl had held hands the entire time, much to the young wolf's chagrin. If it had been an hour later, the young girl might not have survived. They had made it. The young wolf would never have to ponder over the taste of her flesh or if it were possible to eat human teeth - no, he was able to drag her up to his grandparents' home where he would hopefully be able to end his and his family's hunger for years to come.

He gripped the girl's hand and dragged her up to the home, not noting the way she tugged back or dug her weak little heels into the ground. He was too preoccupied with the sight in front of him, of all the wonderful prospects and the food. Oh, the food. His mouth was already salivating, and at any other time he would've been embarrassed, worried about becoming one of those desperate wolves, but the food was too close for him to care.

It wasn't until he had made it up to the front door that he knew something was wrong.

He called, hesitantly, "Grandma?"

He knocked once and called, "Grandpa?"

No answers.

He tugged on the doorknob, but found it was lodged in the frame. He dropped the girl's hand and knocked a bit more forceful before calling, "Grandma? Grandpa?"

There was still no answer. What was once excitement and hunger evolved quickly into fear. The young wolf took a second to wipe the drying saliva, now cold, from his maw before swallowing and rushing to the back of the house where he hoped to find fields of vegetables. When he rounded the corner of the house, he was met with fields and fields of dirt mounds, ash, and rot. He stood still, taking it all in for one second, two, three - all in silence before dropping to his knees and crawling over to the field closest to the house.

He dug his paws into the nearest pile of rot, shoveling it and pressing it into his maw where he swallowed it all. Though his stomach groaned with relief, his throat strained to carry the soured fruit and ash down, and his mouth felt gritty once it had emptied. His hunger had been sated, but the fear and desperation clawed much deeper than his stomach. The young wolf looked back at the girl, who watched, smiling, by the corner of the house. She didn't say anything and neither did he, but his eyes locked on that smile. The way it barely opened her mouth to reveal the graying gums and the little black nubs. The way her tongue, like a black snake, seemed to peek out at him. All of the worry he had over his control evaporated into the air and smelled as rotten as the fields around him.

It wasn't *his* control he feared, and as soon as the thought came to mind, the girl's face contorted. With a battle cry, she reached into her little basket and pulled out a club - a savage little weapon made from a branch and a stone. She rushed him, and his arms were little defense as she clobbered them down and away from his head. He prayed for his family, for himself, and for his life. All he received back was darkness.

When he awoke, it wasn't in his grandparents' house. The world blurred in and out of focus, but he could still pick out the pale forms hovering around, one which he recognized immediately - the red hooded girl. He tried to blink, to lift his hands and to clear his eyes, but found their mangled forms too heavy to lift. All he could manage was writhing and whimpering, a poor showing for a wolf his age. His head throbbed, his body ached, and his fur matted to his body from the sticky air.

The people around him milled about, smacking their gums and rubbing their hands. The little girl pushed her way forward, closest to him, and wafting the scent of rot. The smell sent a wave of nausea through him, and it took all he had not to wretch. He whimpered loudly and this seemed to please the people as they laughed and shifted around – a single hive mind. The little girl giggled loudest of all.

"We're all so hungry. It's too hard to follow the food chain when you're at the bottom. No fruits, no vegetables, all the small animals have been eaten or have died off, but there are plenty who would eat us. Who says we can't eat them first?"

The people around her seemed to close in, creating an impenetrable wall. They gnashed their teeth and even growled. The young wolf could barely tell them apart from the desperate wolves. There was much more to fear than his own species' desperation. Then the little girl lifted what the wolf immediately recognized as the club, and she whispered,

"Good night, little wolf."

Then down the club came, and the wolf was covered in red, as bright as the little girl's hood.

4 – HER NAILS

She picked her nails when she was nervous. It was a habit I both loved and hated. She would pick her nails when I asked her what she wanted for dinner and she would hum, hum, hum. Then her nails would click thump, thump, thump. She was indecisive — another characteristic I had grown to love and hate.

We hardly argued, mainly because she could never decide which side of the argument she wanted to be on.

"I don't want to go dancing," I said.

"But I want to dance," she said.

Then she would hum, bite her lip, then thump, thump, thump.

"But I don't want to sweat," she said.

Thump, thump, thump.

"But sweating is good for the skin, I read that in a magazine," she said.

Thump, thump, thump.

We never did go dancing, so I guess I won in the end.

Every argument and non-argument went the same way for as long as we have been together. She had grown so used to humming that I swore she would do it in her sleep. I would open my eyes in the darkness and catch snippets of show tunes we might have heard on the television before bed, when we non-argued about what show to watch. It wasn't until a few weeks after that she began to thump, thump, thump in her sleep, too.

I would lay awake, waiting for her to stop, but it never did. Thump, thump, thump in the darkness, then thump, thump, thump in the morning when the sun would shine through our windows with shades two different colors. She could never decide which color she liked more. She would be laying on her back, eyes shut, lips tucked into one another as she hummed, and her nails would thump, thump, thump.

The tip of her nail would dig into the cuticle of her thumb on the opposite hand. Once she had cleared it, she would switch hands. It had come to a point where her nails bled through the night. We had to buy new sheets, but she could never decide between cream or white. I bought both just so she would stop thumping, but she never did. The thumping continued, and eventually the cream and the white didn't matter anymore because they were both spotted red.

It had gone on for years, the thump, thump, thumping, and I hadn't slept in all those years. The thumping was invading my thoughts, my daily life. I found myself thumping on my desk at work, I would thump my toes on the inside of my boots, and the thump even seemed to invade my eyelids. Every time they closed, it was with a thump. I couldn't eat, I couldn't sleep, I couldn't live without the thump, thump, thump.

The thumping ended last week.

She was thumping in her sleep again, and I could barely hear her humming over it. I got out of bed and slipped into the hall where I walked to our kitchen. It took me a while, but I eventually found the set of pliers. She had moved the drawers around again. This setup was supposed to be more ergonomic. I think she read that in an article online.

I took the pliers back to the bedroom, and I didn't have to turn on the lights to know where the thumping was. Her hands moved in the darkness like two black smudges, and all the while they thump, thump, thumped. I climbed back in on my side of the bed, then rolled over until I was on top of her. I felt her groan in her chest, and she said,

"No. Not tonight, honey."

I didn't say anything back, and for a while I just lay there, pleased with the sudden silence. In time, the thumping returned, but not until it had been preceded with her usual hum.

I grabbed one of her hands while the other uselessly flailed around, trying to pick and pluck and thump, thump, thump the missing nail. I stabbed the plier blindly until her nail clamped between the two teeth. Her humming stopped. She was awake.

Still, I gripped the nail of her index finger and yanked. She screamed. It was a glorious sound compared to the humming. Finally, something other than humming. She yanked her hand, but it only helped in yanking the nail from its bed. There was hot liquid on my face, sweat and blood from what I could tell. I did each individual fingernail the same way, stabbing blindly at her hand until the teeth clamped down on the nail of her thumb. I pulled at the nail and wiggled it loose from the bed, but the nail ripped in two and only half came free. I clamped down on the last piece, all the while she yanked and jerked and screamed beneath me. It was wonderful.

I repeated the process on both hands. She had stopped

screaming after the third nail. The rest of the time she wept, and as she wept, I could hear the hum still thrumming in her voice. As her hand slipped, slick with blood, from my hand, I pushed myself up until I was sitting on her chest. I could barely see her shift her head as she gasped for breath. In that instance, I gripped her chin, and she immediately began to shake, but I held fast. She stopped her shaking, panted, then said,

"Why are you doing this?"

I didn't respond. As soon as her words clipped, I plunged the pliers into her mouth and caught the bulk of her tongue between their teeth. Then, I pulled. Her screaming, garbled by the stretching and bleeding of her tongue, echoed throughout our bedroom. I was just so damn glad to be rid of the humming, I didn't mind the spray of warmth across my lips. I pulled and pulled, the tension stretching, loosening, then snapping free until the gooey meat hung between the teeth of pliers. She squirmed and shook underneath me in silence for only a few minutes before going still.

I rolled off of her body and onto my side of the bed. All the world was silent, and it was wonderful. I slept with the pliers pressed close to my chest that night. I didn't wake once.

5 – MY BEST FRIEND

I have had one true friend my entire life. I wouldn't consider myself a hermit, more of a shadow – a simple being who would love nothing more than to pass the day just drifting - alone and in silence. I went through all of grade school in that way. People make me claustrophobic. No social life gave way for more study time, and I was a good pupil. I even managed to get into college, despite my pleas to the contrary.

My mother said, "You have too much potential to waste away in your bedroom! What would your father say if he saw you acting like this?"

I wouldn't know. He killed himself. I didn't mind it too much. He worked hard, too hard sometimes, and eventually wore his body out. Once he had worn out the body, next was the brain. His brain turned on him. He went outside, .22 caliber pistol in hand, and shot himself. My mother coped with it by ignoring it all together, instead busying herself with telling the family, preparing the funeral, picking a coffin, flowers, and starting a book club. My mother was good at ignoring things that made her upset. She ignored me a lot. I didn't mind. I coped by going inward.

Still, I was happy. Life was good, and I would be at the state University in the fall. I still didn't know what major I would be. I opted for business because that's where every adviser put kids like me - kids without a reason for being there. Kids whose parents made them go.

It was that fall, in my very first marketing class, I met him. He sat in the very back of the room, only a seat away from the back left corner. It was fate that I had chosen that seat for myself. I sat down and the kid leaned over.

"Hey!" he said.

His voice was loud and high-pitched, a voice which drew the attention of the room toward us. I could already tell I was going to hate him. I tried to ignore him, hoping he would give up and leave me alone. I kept my eyes on my desk and tried to focus on digging the point of my pencil into the particle wood.

It was for naught. He leaned even further toward my

desk, nearly lifting himself out of his own seat. The proximity had me curling in on myself. I hated him.

"Hey! My name's Joshua. What year are you?"

I remember rolling my eyes and grumbling to him. I was a freshman. We were in a freshman class. Why did he have to waste my time with such trivial questions? I told him as coldly as I could manage, "Freshman."

While it didn't deter him in the least, I had hoped it would at least sate him enough to give me peace. If anything, it only encouraged him further. I remember his eyes growing wide like saucers - two beautiful blue orbs burrowing into me. His mouth opened into an "O" and he let out a small sound of surprise.

"Wow. You look so much older than me. Have you failed a lot?"

He was stupid, there was no denying that. I wasn't the friendliest of people, but I knew better than to speak so bluntly to a complete stranger. I didn't even try to play along. I turned my face back toward the front of the classroom, praying the teacher would come in and start the class. I remember seeing Joshua fidgeting in his seat and leaning - toward me, back to his seat, toward me, back to his seat. He was giving me hives. Thankfully, the teacher made it to class, and Joshua's attention shifted from me to her. He settled down into his seat, and I was once again at peace.

The teacher called roll, and when my name came along, she stuttered, which made the whole room erupt with laughter. I decided then that I hated everyone in there, too.

"P-Poppy?"

I just raised my hand. The teacher apologized and chuckled to herself, her round form shaking with glee. She wasn't sorry. I was beginning to hate everything, University included, then Joshua leaned my way again.

"Poppy? Like the flower?"

I looked at him, and he was smiling. Something about his smile seemed so much more genuine than any other I had seen. It invited me in and from then on, I grew more and more comfortable with our relationship. The guy still annoyed me, and I hated him and his stupid questions, but he was always happy. He smiled at everyone we passed and thanked every bus driver, cashier, and gardener we came in contact with. That kind of positivity is addictive. It leaves a stain on a person, and I will never forget it as long as I live.

As the semester went on and on, I learned more about the boy I called my best friend. He wasn't really a boy, for one. He was a grown man, a twenty-five year old man, much to my surprise. He was taking every class offered at the University, even ones that weren't required for his major, which was Fine Art. He loved to draw, flowers being his favorite. He would paint pictures of poppy flowers as often as he could. The little red buds he would smudge on paper and canvas were beautiful, but the mass of them he pumped out every week was nauseating. I would often take the pictures back to my house where I would then take a black marker and mark everything out until the page was a wall of black. It broke the monotony of the other fifty poppy paintings I had scattered around my room.

We didn't do much in the way of "hanging out," except for the occasional nights I spent at his house and the times we would smoke his weed. It was when smoked that his positivity sagged. He told me about how poor his family was, how he was in debt from all of his schooling, how he would never get a job, and how he wished he had done more with his life. On one of those nights, after a particularly emotional vent, I kissed him. He kissed me back, but we never got the chance to do it again. The next day, he told me he had been diagnosed with cancer, just a few months prior to starting the fall semester. His tumor was inoperable.

We couldn't hang out on campus anymore, and he had been confined to a room in a hospital. I quit going to class so I could spend time with him. I didn't tell my mother. I would go there every day, then sleep at my house where I would then wake up and go straight back to the hospital. I eventually just stopped going home. He lost his hair in chunks. He kept telling me he would get better and it would grow back. I just called him a dumbass. Even as he grew weaker and weaker, and his hands shook any time he picked something up, he kept trying to paint those damn poppies.

I remember the day he died better than I remember the day my father died. My father's death was impersonal, held no meaning to me. It was just cloudy the day he died. It rained the day Joshua died. Joshua was mine. He had been my only friend, and all I had to show for it was those damn poppy pictures. I could still hear his voice in my head as he breathed his last breath. He looked at me, eyes glassy and strained. He smiled and asked that stupid question,

"Poppy? Like the flower, right?"

I hated him. I hated him more than I had ever hated anyone in my entire life. Only his parents attended the funeral, excluding me, and they left before the coffin was covered. I stayed and watched. I stayed even after that. I stayed even though it began to rain, after the workers and the caretakers had left. Then, I got a shovel, and I started digging. Through the mud, the filth, the worms - I dug until metal hit wood. I uncovered his coffin and lifted the lid. He looked like he was sleeping. I reached in and gripped the collar of his red speckled, white shirt. I shook him.

"Wake up."

The red specks reminded me of the poppies. I tried to pull him out of the box, but his body was too stiff. There was no way I could take him with me. There was no way I could take *all* of him with me. I laid him back in the coffin, then lifted the shovel. I raised it over my head then dropped it, cutting into Joshua's neck with a satisfying crunch. I lifted the shovel again, then brought it down, missing the mark and hacking at another section. I chopped again and again and again until his neck was nothing but a pulpy mess. I reached down and cradled him in my hands.

"You're an idiot, Joshua."

He felt cold.

I took him home with me. I kept Joshua's head pressed close to my chest where he could keep warm. He was always so frail. I didn't want him to catch a cold. I took him to my room where I laid him down on my pillow. His pulpy neck leaked a watery, pink fluid. I sighed and rubbed his bald head.

"Get some sleep. You'll feel better in the morning."

Then, I got into bed, pressing my face against his cold

cheek.

Joshua is mine. He is *my* best friend.

6 – THE ASH MAN

The Coaling, Alabama Police Department Records:

January 19, 1993,

Following the case of the disappearance of Coal, Alabama, the only evidence of the town were a series of calls over four days starting on January 19. The following is a transcription of those calls.

The first call came at approximately 9:15 a.m. from a Jessica Gamble. Officer James Montgomery answered.

"Coaling Police Department, how can I assist you?"

A panicked voice on the other end is somewhat muffled by static.

"Officer? Are you an officer?"

Unidentifiable voices can be heard in the background. They are lost behind static.

"Yes, this is Officer Montgomery, what is it?"

"There is a man in our yard."

"Ma'am where are you located?"

Mrs. Gamble says something away from the receiver. Officer Montgomery, upon further questioning, insists she said, "Is he still there?"

"Coal, Alabama-"

Montgomery sighs.

"Ma'am, it will be best if you call your local police department. If you don't know the number, 9-1-1 can dispatch someone. They'll get to you much quicker."

Mrs. Gamble makes a grumbling noise.

"I can't get a hold of anyone there. Y'all are one town over. Can't you do anything?"

Before the officer can respond, Mrs. Gamble is heard speaking to the other voices in the background. Mrs. Gamble continues to speak into the receiver.

"What? Is he at the door? What is he doing? Tell him to go away!"

At this point, Officer Montgomery tries to interject.

"Ma'am, it would be best if you keep the door closed. Turn off all lights and wait until he leaves. I'll contact the Coal-"

At this point, Mrs. Gamble's phone loses service. The line is alive, but there is only a wall of static. Officer Montgomery continues to try and keep in contact with Mrs. Gamble, but the phone call disconnects some time later.

The second call came in at 1:31 p.m. The caller was Mrs. Gamble again, but the call was connected to Officer Michael Hansen.

"Coaling Police Department, this is-"

Mrs. Gamble interrupts.

"Officer Montgomery? Is this Montgomery?"

Montgomery had already gone home for the evening, and Officer Hansen was unable to patch her over to him.

"Ma'am, Officer Montgomery has gone home. What can I do for-"

"Whoever you are, I am at 13 Melody Street, Coal, Alabama. Not Coaling, Coal."

"Ma'am, perhaps it's best if you call the Coal-"

Mrs. Gamble makes a frustrated noise.

"How many times do I have to say it?"

Mrs. Gamble loses service for a second before

returning.

"Just come. He's writing things on our windows!"

"Who is? Ma'am let me patch you over to the police department-"

Mrs. Gamble begins to scream. Much of what she says is unintelligible, but what is transcribed is what the receiver was able to pick up.

"Why? How are you doing this? Dark! It's so dark!"

Static.

"Ma'am? Ma'am? Are you alright? I'm sending officers now. Just stay calm. 13 Melody Street, right?"

The call disconnects.

After the second call, Officer Hansen was able to alert the rest of the department, and assembled a group of five or six officers. Hansen attempted to contact the Coal Police Department, but there was no ring. No dial tone. Hansen didn't try to call again. The officers, including Hansen, traveled down to Tingle Tangle Road, the only way to get to Coal, Alabama. The road has three entrances: two in Vance, Alabama, the other in Coaling. Coal was named after the coal mines from which the town was founded, and Coaling spawned off as an urban version of its roots.

There were still people living in Coal, the population dwindling over the past couple of years. Coal was down to six hundred people since the last census, and it was filled with coal miners, their wives, and their children, who would one day be destined to join their fathers in the coal mines. It was the way of Coal, Alabama.

Hansen and his group of officers took Tingle Tangle, in search of Melody Street. The road was named Tingle Tangle with good reason. It wasn't a long road, six or seven miles, but it was a never-ending twist of turns and curves, which made travel much slower than the officers would've liked. There was a reason Coal had its own separate police force. It was too hard to get into Coal from the outside, and the dump trucks traveling from the mines had created potholes and worn down the shoulders of the road. It was dangerous, but Hansen and his squad drove in as quickly as they could.

They searched up and down Tingle Tangle for Melody street, but it was as if they had blinked their eyes and in that second, they had ended up at the end of the road, just outside of Vance. It was as if the entire squad had fallen asleep from Coaling to Vance, and as they trekked back to the station, each officer reported the same experience. It was as if they had blinked and missed the entire thing.

Hansen attempted to phone the Coal Police Department again, but there was still no answer.

At 10:12 p.m. the Coaling Police Department received another call, this one originating from an officer of the Vance Police Department. Hansen remained on duty in case any other calls arrived from Mrs. Gamble, and he took the call from Vance.

"Coaling Police Department, Officer Hansen speaking."

Someone clears their throat.

"Officer Hansen, this is Tyler Wells of the Vance PD. We've been receiving disturbing calls from the Coal area. Reports of a man trespassing people's yards, and of the Coal PD being unreachable. You've received similar calls?"

"Yes. One, but we went out to see what was going on, and . . . Well."

There is a lengthy silence.

"Well what? What was out there?"

"It's hard to say. We didn't see anything."

Officer Wells sighs.

"So it was a prank?"

"No, no. Not like that. I mean, we literally saw nothing. One moment we were on our way to Coal, the next we were in Vance. It was as if we had slept through the whole thing."

"Hansen, I'm assuming you're a great officer, but what you're saying doesn't make any sense. You can't just blink past an entire town. What about the mines? Did you see them?"

"No. No mines."

"Were you even paying any attention?"

"Yes, yes. Well . . . I assume we were."

"You assume? Our department doesn't rely on assumptions, Hansen."

Hansen sighs.

"Look. I know what I saw, and I know what I didn't see. I didn't see Coal. It vanished."

Another sigh.

"Well, my department will be running our own investigation. If you receive any other calls, direct them our way. Wouldn't want to trouble your department any more than it already has been."

Hansen abruptly ends the call.

The situation regarding Coal, Alabama continues into the next day on January 20, 1993. The next call isn't received until 10:00 a.m. from an unidentifiable mobile phone. The call is picked up by Officer Montgomery.

"Hello, this is Coaling Police Department-"

A wall of static barely muffles the man on the other end. He is later identified as Officer Tyler Wells, though there is no hard evidence to confirm this account.

"Hansen? Is Hansen there?"

"Sir, if you'll just tell me your name, I can patch you over to him."

"No time. You were right. Coal is gone."

Muffled cries.

"No, no. That's not right either. It's not gone. It's here, but it's in darkness. Don't look in."

"Sir, we'll be sending out a team to come find you, is there anything there? Anything that might let us know where you are?"

The static gets louder and the man begins to yell.

"Don't come! Stay away from Coal! The ash!"

The phone call disconnects.

Montgomery attempted to call back, but the phone number was no longer in service. Officer Tyler Wells and ten men from the Vance PD have since been classified as missing. No other calls were received from the Vance PD and all calls from Coal were immediately patched over to the Coaling Police Department.

January 22, 1993, the next call arrived from Coal around 10:15 a.m. Officer Montgomery has been designated as lead officer in all cases regarding Coal, Alabama.

"Yes? This is Officer Montgomery."

There is heavy static.

"Hello?"

The static continues, but another voice also jumps in.

"The children have gone."

"Children? What about the children?"

The woman on the other end screams.

"We told them not to go outside! We told them! But the Ash man... The Ash man got them."

Officer Montgomery tries to interject.

"Ma'am what is your name? Who is the Ash man-"

The woman begins screaming again.

"He covered us all in darkness! All of us! He lures us with his voice! He is the voice of the devil!

He took Jonathan!"

The woman begins to weep.

"My Jonathan..."

The static clears for an instant, just long enough for Montgomery to pick up a loud banging sound. The woman gasps and begins to sob.

"Oh God... Oh God... He's coming. He's coming for me..."

"Who is? Ma'am?"

The woman shushes Montgomery in between sobs.

"Hush... hush... He can hear us all... He's coming for me. He wants me to be with Jonathan."

Montgomery whispers into the phone.

"Ma'am, remain calm. Can you find a safe place? Can you cover the windows?"

The woman is silent for a while, then begins to laugh.

"Cover the windows? Cover the windows? Safe place? Coal is gone, officer. We are the capital of Hell!"

The woman sobs as she laughs.

"It's too dark to see, too dark to hide... There is no place safe anymore. The Ash man is Satan. He will find us all."

Before Montgomery can respond, the call abruptly ends. Montgomery attempts to call back, but the phone has been disconnected. No other calls come in for the remainder of the day.

The very same day at 3:07 p.m. the final call from Coal, Alabama is received by Officer Montgomery. The following transcription is the final account from any residents in the town. The case has been closed ever since.

"Hello? Hello? This is Officer Montgomery. Hello?"

The same static is heard, and the voice of the same woman earlier whispers.

"Jonathan is back..."

"Ma'am? Is that you? Your son is back? Is he alright?"

The woman sobs on the other end.

"All the children are back... but they're not."

"What do you mean?"

The woman hiccups and continues to sob, whispering into the receiver.

"They aren't them anymore... They knock on the doors and the windows, begging us to be let in..."

"Then let them in! They're your children!"

The woman yells.

"No they're not!"

She sobs again before continuing to whisper.

"The Ash man has changed them... Jonathan does not cry, he does not laugh or smile. I ask him questions and he laughs. He laughs then tells me to let him in. He is not my son..."

The static clears long enough for Montgomery to hear knocking. The woman on the other end screams, then sobs, whispering frantically into the receiver.

"Oh God. He's still there. He's outside but he won't leave."

She begins to weep, much louder than before.

"He calls me 'mommy.'"

Officer Montgomery tries to calm her.

"Hush, hush. Please stay calm ma'am. Are you hiding? Can you hide somewhere?"

The woman breathes in before she responds, whispering,

"Yes, yes... I'm in the closet. I locked the doors. He can't get in."

The static clears up again, and a distant voice can be heard.

"Mommy?"

The woman gasps and begins to sob.

"Mommy? Mommy? Where are you? Can I come in

now mommy? The dust is getting into my eyes."

The woman sobs louder, all the while Montgomery tries to keep her calm on his end. Then, a loud crash and the breaking of glass can be heard. The woman screams into the receiver and can be heard shuffling.

"Oh God! He's broken a window! He's broken a window!"

"Ma'am, ma'am! You have to be quiet! Please, keep calm-"

Muffled footsteps, determined to be from a distance, step calmly and quietly toward the woman's location.

"Mommy? Where are you? I miss you."

The woman sobs. Then there is complete silence. Montgomery starts to speak, but stops as the sound of a creaking door is heard. The laughter of a child fills the silence.

"I found you."

The call abruptly ends.

Those were the final moments recorded and transcribed from the case regarding the disappearance of Coal, Alabama. A few weeks following the final call, multiple search parties went out for the missing people and the town, but all returned with the same description: It was like they blinked, and the road ended. There was no way in and no way out of Coal, Alabama. After a while, people stopped searching, and the missing persons reports no longer came in. What remained of them was eventually added to the cold case of Coal. Nearly 600 people, five mines, and part of a police squad just vanished into thin air.

The towns of Vance and Coaling built up a few more mines along what remained of Tingle Tangle road, and on some occasions, the workers report hearing the voices of children within the ash. They laugh and they call out, "Mommy?" but their reports are considered superstition.

To my readers,

Thank you so much for picking up a copy of *The Mind, the Body*. While I wish I could take the time to thank you all individually, I unfortunately can't. As I sit at my desk and write this to you all, my heart is heavy with gratitude and appreciation. You don't realize how much this means to me, to have your support. Without you, I wouldn't be living this dream.

Now I must ask one more favor. While I can't take the time to thank each individual person who reads this, I can read what each person thinks of this book and the stories within. Whether you loved it, hated it, whatever, I would love to know what you think. Please feel free to leave a review on whatever site you would like. Reviews are important to authors everywhere. It lets us know what you want more of and whether we should keep writing.

Keep supporting your authors and keep leaving feedback. We'll love you even more for it.

Love,

Alyssa Hubbard

ABOUT THE AUTHOR

Alyssa Hubbard is author to *Humans and Their Creations*, *An Austrian March*, and the *Apocalyptia* series. Her poetry has been featured in *Crack the Spine* and *scissors & spackle*. She was born in a small town in Alabama, where she spent more time writing and reading than playing outside. Her sister is a two-time cancer survivor, and she is her greatest inspiration. She attends the University of Alabama for a BA in English with a minor in Creative Writing. Alyssa spends most of her time reading, writing, re-writing, and re-writing, and re-writing, and re-writing... She loves blogging and singing in public. Follow her if you dare.

Find out more at:
www.LissyWrites.com

Made in the USA
Charleston, SC
12 March 2015